This book belongs to

_____

This book is dedicated to my children - Mikey, Kobe, and Jojo.

Copyright © 2023 Grow Grit Press LLC. All rights reserved. No part of this book may be reproduced in any form without permission in writing from the publisher. Please send bulk order requests to info@ninjalifehacks.tv

Paperback ISBN: 978-1-63731-724-2
Hardcover ISBN: 978-1-63731-726-6
eBook ISBN: 978-1-63731-725-9

Printed and bound in the USA.
NinjaLifeHacks.tv

Ninja Life Hacks®
by Mary Nhin

5   6   7   8

13   14   15

19   20   21

24   25

Ninja Life Hacks
NUMBERS

By Mary Nhin

A ninja knows about numbers,
Would you like to count along?

Come on, let's count to **25**,
It shouldn't take too long!

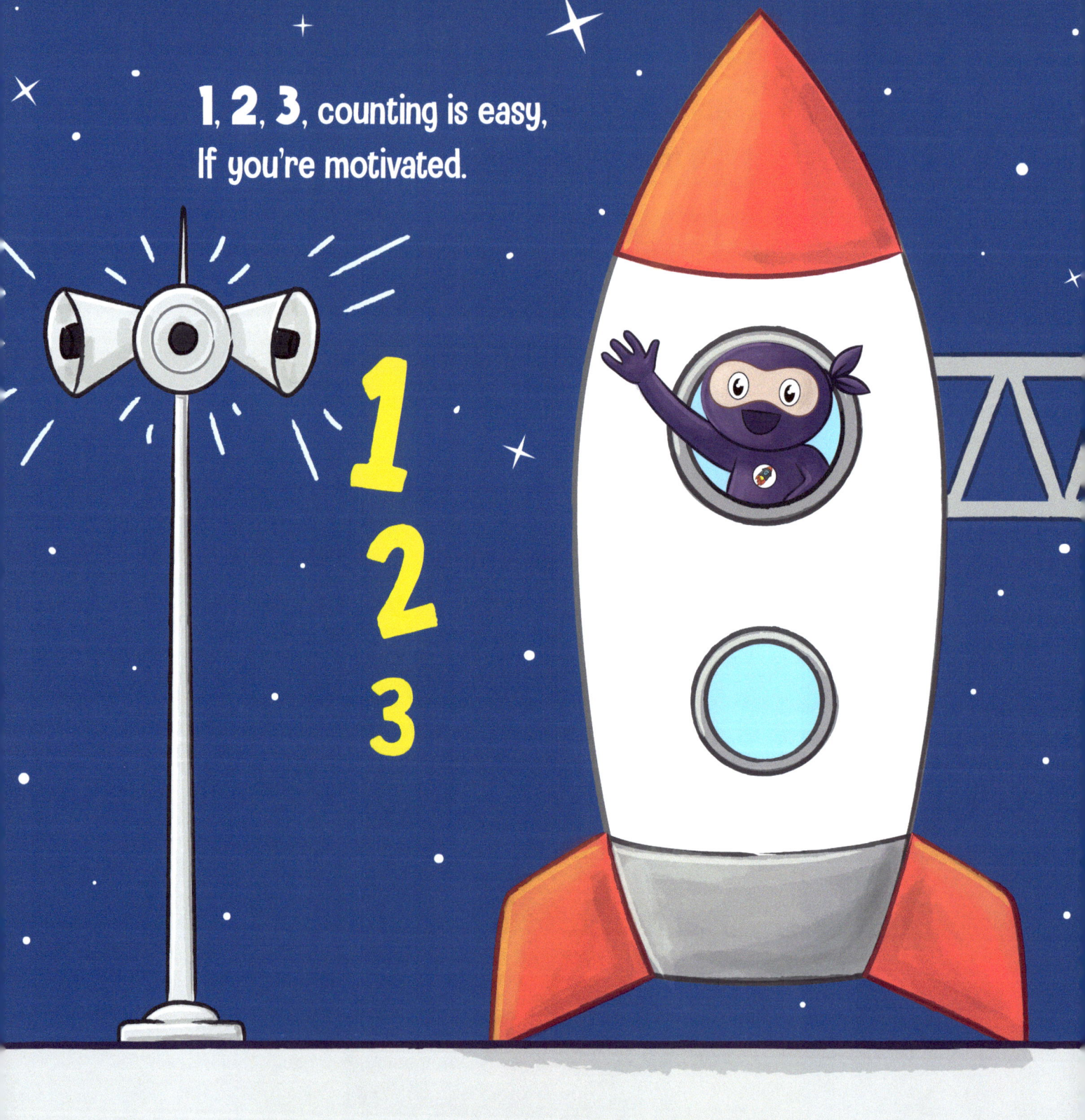

Next up in our numbers
Are **7**, **8**, and **9**.
When a teacher or classmate helps you count,
It shows they're being kind.

10, 11, 12, keep going,
You have lots of support.

13, 14, 15, that's great,
You're such a wonderful sport!

Ok, now let's take a break,
We're already in the teens.

And mastering counting can be **fun**,
Even if it isn't what it seems.

Before you move on to more numbers,
Count the bubbles out first.
There are many more numbers to count to,
If you're **curious**, go to the next verse!

16 and **17** are next on the list,
We're inching closer to 20!

If we were counting **money**,
Rest assured, you would have plenty!

Counting upward shows a **growth mindset**
Which is a great thing, didn't you know?

FINALLY, we're at **20**, but stay focused,
We're still counting for more.

Be **confident** we can get to 25,
Before counting becomes a bore.

And do you know what number comes next?
If you're **curious**, we're almost done.

That's right, good work, you guessed correctly.
Next comes **21**.

And now we're up to **22**
And right after that? **23**!

As long as you're **self-disciplined**,
Counting is easy, you see!

24 is next, don't be **nervous**,
We're almost at the end.

Once we're done with all your counting,
Be **kind** and **share** this book with a friend.

OK, you know our final number,
That's right! It's **25**.

You did it, and it was **perfect**!
Now how about a high-five?

Continue the learning with our fun lesson plans which include superpower skills practice, STEM activity, craft, and more! Visit ninjalifehacks.tv

@marynhin @officialninjalifehacks
#NinjaLifeHacks

Ninja Life Hacks

Mary Nhin   Ninja Life Hacks

@officialninjalifehacks

13 14 15

19 20 21

24 25

www.ingramcontent.com/pod-product-compliance
Lightning Source LLC
Chambersburg PA
CBHW041524070526
44585CB00002B/79